Dear Parents and Educators,

Welcome to Penguin Young Readers! As parents and educators, you know that each child develops at his or her own pace—in terms of speech, critical thinking, and, of course, reading. Penguin Young Readers recognizes this fact. As a result, each Penguin Young Readers book is assigned a traditional easy-to-read level (1–4) as well as a Guided Reading Level (A–P). Both of these systems will help you choose the right book for your child. Please refer to the back of each book for specific leveling information. Penguin Young Readers features esteemed authors and illustrators, stories about favorite characters, fascinating nonfiction, and more!

Young Cam Jansen and the Spotted Cat Mystery

This book is perfect for a **Transitional Reader** who:

- can read multisyllable and compound words;
- can read words with prefixes and suffixes;
- is able to identify story elements (beginning, middle, end, plot, setting, characters, problem, solution); and
- can understand different points of view.

Here are some **activities** you can do during and after reading this book:

- Creative Writing: Pretend you are one of the students in Ms. Dee's class. On a sheet of paper, make a poster for the lost cat. Include details such as a description of the cat and where the owner can find his/her cat.
- List all the words in the story that have an -ed ending. Write the root word next to each word with an -ed ending. The chart below will get you started.

word with an -ed ending	root word
chased	chase
dropped	drop
purred	purr

Remember, sharing the love of reading with a child is the best gift you can give!

—Bonnie Bader, EdM
Penguin Young Readers program

*Penguin Young Readers are leveled by independent reviewers applying the standards developed by Irene Fountas and Gay Su Pinnell in *Matching Books to Readers: Using Leveled Books in Guided Reading*, Heinemann, 1999.

For Netanel, Emunah, Avital,
and Techiya—DA

To Ding-guo, Sue-Hwa, Qing, Jeff, and
Stephanie—SN

Penguin Young Readers
Published by the Penguin Group
Penguin Group (USA) Inc., 375 Hudson Street, New York, New York 10014, USA
Penguin Group (Canada), 90 Eglinton Avenue East, Suite 700, Toronto, Ontario M4P 2Y3, Canada
(a division of Pearson Penguin Canada Inc.)
Penguin Books Ltd, 80 Strand, London WC2R 0RL, England
Penguin Ireland, 25 St Stephen's Green, Dublin 2, Ireland (a division of Penguin Books Ltd)
Penguin Group (Australia), 707 Collins Street, Melbourne, Victoria 3008, Australia
(a division of Pearson Australia Group Pty Ltd)
Penguin Books India Pvt Ltd, 11 Community Centre, Panchsheel Park, New Delhi—110 017, India
Penguin Group (NZ), 67 Apollo Drive, Rosedale, Auckland 0632, New Zealand
(a division of Pearson New Zealand Ltd)
Penguin Books, Rosebank Office Park, 181 Jan Smuts Avenue, Parktown North 2193, South Africa
Penguin China, B7 Jaiming Center, 27 East Third Ring Road North,
Chaoyang District, Beijing 100020, China

Penguin Books Ltd, Registered Offices: 80 Strand, London WC2R 0RL, England

 First published in 2006 by Viking and in 2007 by Puffin Books, imprints of Penguin Group (USA) Inc. Published in 2013 by Penguin Young Readers, an imprint of Penguin Group (USA) Inc., 345 Hudson Street, New York, New York 10014. Manufactured in China.

The Library of Congress has cataloged the Viking edition
under the following Control Number: 2005034006

ISBN 978-0-14-241012-7 10 9 8 7 6 5 4 3 2

PENGUIN YOUNG READERS

LEVEL 3
TRANSITIONAL READER

Young Cam Jansen
and the Spotted Cat Mystery

by David A. Adler
illustrated by Susanna Natti

Penguin Young Readers
An Imprint of Penguin Group (USA) Inc.

Contents

Chapter 1
Meow! Meow!

"Please, wipe your boots on the mat," Mrs. Wayne, the principal's assistant, called out.

It was a cold, rainy day.

Cam Jansen and her friend Eric Shelton walked into school.

They wiped their boots on the mat.

"Aren't you that clicking girl?" Mrs. Wayne asked.

Cam smiled. "I say, 'Click!' when

I want to remember something."

Eric told Mrs. Wayne,

"Cam remembers whatever she sees.

It's as if she has a camera in her head.

That's why she says, 'Click!'

That's the sound a camera makes."

"Turn around," Mrs. Wayne told Cam.

"Tell me what I'm wearing."

Cam turned.

"Click!" she said, and closed her eyes.

"You're wearing boots."

"Of course I am," Mrs. Wayne said.
"It's cold and raining outside."
"There's an oak leaf on the toe
of your left boot," Cam said.
"The tip of the leaf is torn."

Mrs. Wayne looked at her boot.
"Oh my! You're right," she said.
Cam's real name is Jennifer, but
because of her memory, people
called her "the Camera."
Then "the Camera" became just
"Cam."
"You're amazing!" Mrs. Wayne said.

"You really do have a great memory."

Cam opened her eyes.

Then she walked with Eric to class.

Their teacher, Ms. Dee,

was standing in the hall,

right by the door to their classroom.

"Good morning," Ms. Dee said.

"You're the first students here."

"My mom didn't want us to wait in

the rain for the bus," Cam said.

"She drove us today."

"Please," Ms Dee said,

"take off your raincoats and boots."

Cam and Eric walked into the room.

The room was neat.

The floor was clean.

They took off their coats.

They took off their boots.

They went to the back of the room

and hung their coats on hooks.

"Hey," Eric said.

"Look in the corner.

Danny forgot his sweater."

Eric went to pick it up
and something moved.
"Meow! Meow!"
A white cat
with a large black spot on its tail
ran from the corner
and hid beneath Ms. Dee's desk.

Chapter 2
The Cat's Name Is *Spotty*

"Good morning," Beth said
as she walked into the classroom.
Jane, Tim, and Danny walked in, too.
"I love the rain," Danny said.
He spun around.
Water sprayed off his raincoat.
"Hey!" Beth shouted.
"You got me wet!"
"Water is good for you," Danny said.

"It makes plants grow."

"Well, I'm not a plant!"

More children walked into the room.

Danny dropped his books

on the floor.

His homework papers fell out.

He shook his boots.

Water splashed off them

and hit the cat. *"Meow!"*

It ran across Danny's books and

papers, back into Danny's sweater.

"Whose cat is that?" Danny asked.

“We found it here this morning,”

Cam said.

“Oh, how sweet,” Ms. Dee said.

She held out her arms.

“Come here,” she said softly.

The cat looked at Ms. Dee.

“Come here,” Ms. Dee said again.

The cat ran into her arms.

Ms. Dee petted the cat.

Then she told Cam,

"You can't keep a cat in school.

You'll have to call your mother

to come and take it home."

"But it's not my cat," Cam said.

Danny laughed.

He pointed at Cam and sang,

"Cam Jansen has a little cat.

Its fleece is white as snow.

It followed Cam to school one day.

Ms. Dee said it must go."

"That's not funny," Cam said.

"It's not my cat."

"We found it in the coat corner,"
Eric said, "in Danny's sweater."
"Well, it's not my cat," Danny said.
"I don't have any pets."
"Then whose cat is it?" Ms. Dee asked.

No one answered.
"The cat has a collar," Beth said.
Ms. Dee held up the cat.
A small brass tag hung from its collar.
Ms. Dee looked at it and said,
"The cat's name is *Spotty*."

Chapter 3
Something Strange

"I'll make 'Lost Cat' signs,"
Danny said.
Beth said, "First we should give Spotty
something to eat and drink."
"I have a can of tuna for lunch,"
Ms. Dee said.
"I'll share it with Spotty."
Ms. Dee opened her lunch bag and
took out a small can of tuna fish.
Ms. Dee put a sheet of paper
on the floor.

She opened the can.

Then she spilled some tuna fish

onto the paper.

"It's for you," Ms. Dee told Spotty.

Spotty purred.

But Spotty didn't eat the fish.

"I have some water," Eric said.

"And I have a bowl," Ms. Dee added.

Eric took a small bottle of water

from his lunch bag.

Ms. Dee took a bowl from her closet.

She set it beside the tuna fish.

Eric poured some water into the bowl.

Beth stood beside the fish and water.

"Here, Spotty," Beth said.

Spotty didn't run to the food
and water.

It ran into Beth's arms.

Cam looked at Spotty.

Then she looked at Danny's papers.

Cam closed her eyes and said,
"Click!"

"Eat some fish," Beth told Spotty.

"Drink some water."

But Spotty purred.

"I'm done," Danny said.

He held up a sheet of paper.

Are you looking for me?

was on the top of the paper.

Beneath that was a picture.

"That's not Spotty," Beth said.

"It looks like a shoe with feet.

Now who would be looking

for a shoe with feet?"

Cam opened her eyes.

"Look at my sign," Danny said.

Beth said, “Does that look
like Spotty?”
Cam looked at the sign.
“It’s very nice,” Cam said,
“but I don’t think we need that sign.
Look at Danny’s other papers—
the ones on the floor.”
“Hey,” Danny said.
“That’s my homework.”
“There’s something strange
about those papers,” Cam said.
“Something is missing from them.”

Chapter 4
Cam Jansen Clicked!

Danny looked at
his homework papers.
"There's nothing missing," he said.
"I answered every question."
Eric looked at Danny's homework.
"Name the world's five oceans,"
Eric read.
Then he read Danny's answer.
"George, Fred, Nancy, Jacob,
and Beth."
"I'm not an ocean," Beth said.

“The world’s five oceans,” Eric said, “are Atlantic, Pacific, Indian, Arctic, and Antarctic.”

Cam said, “The right answers are not all that’s missing from Danny’s homework.

Spotty walked across those papers. What’s missing are Spotty’s wet paw prints.”

“Yes,” Ms. Dee said.

“I clicked,” Cam said, “and looked at

the picture in my head.
The floor was clean.
If Spotty came here from outside the school, there would have been lots of wet paw prints on the floor."
"Maybe he came in yesterday," Beth said.
"If Spotty came here last night, then he would have been hungry."
Ms. Dee asked Cam, "When do you think Spotty came to school?"
Cam smiled.
"I think Spotty lives in the school."

Chapter 5
The Reward I Want

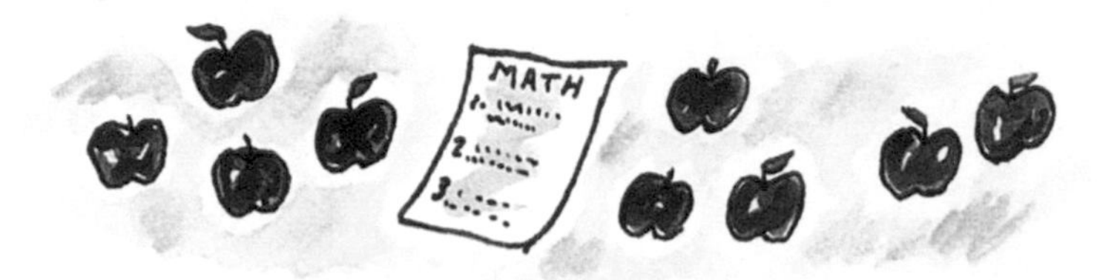

"Let's ask Mrs. Wayne," Eric said.

"She would know if a class
has a pet cat."

"Eric, that's a good idea,"
Ms. Dee said.

"You and Cam should go,
and of course, Beth."

Beth was still holding Spotty.

"What about me?" Danny asked.

Ms. Dee told Danny,
"You need to stay here.

You think there's an ocean
named George."
Cam, Eric, and Beth left the room.
They walked toward the front hall.
Eric said, "The kindergarten classes
have pets.
They have fish and hamsters."
"But they don't have a cat,"
Cam said.
"They wouldn't.
Cats eat fish and hamsters."
Cam stopped.

"Oh my," she said. "That's it."

Cam started to walk the other way.

"Follow me," she said.

They walked to the back hall.

"Cats don't only eat

fish and hamsters.

They eat mice.

Lots of stores have cats

to keep mice away."

Cam stopped at the custodian's door.

She knocked on it.

"Who is it?" Mrs. Adams asked.

"It's me," Cam said, "Cam Jansen."

Cam opened the door.

"Spotty!" Mrs. Adams said.

"Where were you?"

Spotty jumped from Beth

and into Mrs. Adams's arms.

Mrs. Adams told Cam, Eric, and Beth,

"A few years ago, the gym teacher

came in here all upset.

He saw mice in the gym.

That's when I got Spotty.

She chased the mice out.

Now I just love her.

But I'm careful.

Some children are allergic to cats.

I was so busy all morning

mopping up puddles.

I must have left my door open

and Spotty got out."

Beth said, "We found Spotty

in our classroom.

We didn't know how she got there."

"Cam solved the mystery," Eric said.

"Please," Mrs. Adams said,

"take pretzels and juice as a reward."

Cam and Eric each took a pretzel
from the bowl on Mrs. Adams's desk.
"I would like to come here
and visit Spotty," Beth said.

"That's the reward I want."
Spotty purred.
"Spotty and I would like that,"
Mrs. Adams said.
"Visit us after lunch."
There was a knock on the door.
Mrs. Wayne came into the office.

"Some children didn't wipe their feet on the mat," Mrs. Wayne said. "There's a puddle in the front hall." Mrs. Adams told Cam, Eric, and Beth, "I need to go to work." "We need to go to class," Eric said. "I'll walk with you," Mrs. Wayne told the children. When they were in the hall, Mrs. Wayne told Cam, "Now, close your eyes and click!"

Cam closed her eyes and clicked!

"Now," Mrs. Wayne said, "tell me

what Mrs. Adams was wearing.

Tell me about the signs

on her office walls.

Tell me everything

that was on her desk."

Eric and Beth held Cam's hands

as she walked with her eyes closed.

And as she walked,

Cam answered every one

of Mrs. Wayne's questions.

A Cam Jansen Memory Game

Take another look at the picture on page 4.
Study it.
Blink your eyes and say, "Click!"
Then turn back to this page
and answer these questions:

1. What color is Cam's raincoat?
   What color is Eric's?
2. Is Cam carrying an umbrella?
3. Who came into school first,
   Cam or Eric?
4. Is Cam smiling? Is Eric smiling?
5. What color is the floor mat?